This
book belongs
to

Joel Wiegner

With lots & lots of love from
Grandad & GrandE

Christmas 2006

AMAZING
ADVENTURES

REED PUBLISHING (NZ) LTD
TE KARUHI TĀ TĀPUI O REED (AOTEAROA)
Established in 1907, Reed is New Zealand's largest
book publisher, with over 600 titles in print.
www.reed.co.nz

Published by Reed Children's Books, a division of Reed Publishing (NZ) Ltd,
39 Rawene Road, Birkenhead, Auckland 0626. Associated companies, branches
and representatives throughout the world.

A catalogue entry for this book is available from the
National Library of New Zealand.

ISBN 13: 978 1 86978 004 3
ISBN 10: 1 86978 004 3
First published 2006

Designed by Suzanne Wesley

Printed in China by Nordica

Witi Ihimaera

The Amazing Adventures of Razza the Rat

Illustrated by Astrid Matijasevich

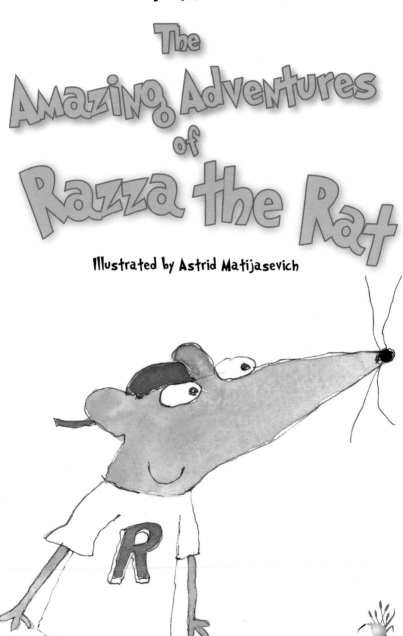

REED

Part One

There once was a rat called RAZZA who was a very
adventurous fella. He loved to tie
a knot in the tail of a cat. Or steal
cheese from a trap set up to
catch a rat. His best trick was
scaring women (or men) where
they sat. What fun to hear
them shriek and jump off the mat!
Could anything be funnier than that?

'That young Razza,' the rat elders said, 'will come to no good,' and they each shook their head.

Well, girls and boys, remember as you play with your toys, sometimes if you gamble you come off the worst.

Do you know that saying, 'Curiosity killed the cat'? The same can apply to a curious rat.

One night, Razza saw a most interesting sight. It looked like a box with **NO LOCK** and was white.

'I WONDER WHAT'S INSIDE?' RAZZA ASKED.

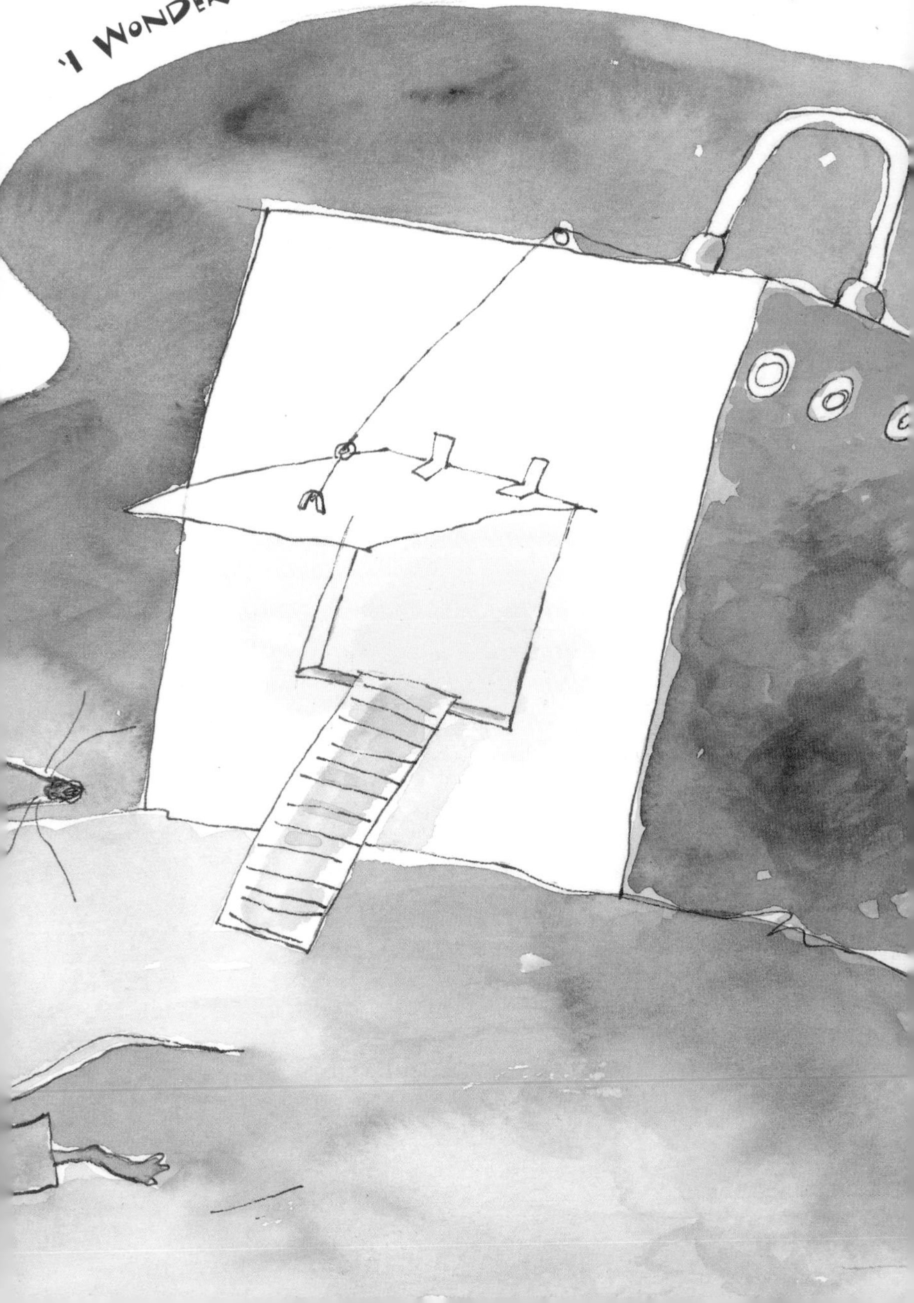

With one mighty spring he jumped through the flap.
With an almighty snap he was caught in the trap.

'**Oh, bother, bother, belly button!**' he said.

'See? What did we say?' the rat elders asked, as they
watched the box bob down the street and away.
'Stay in your mouse holes, children, stay, because
this is what happens to young rats who stray.'

Luckily for Razza, his captors **didn't** want him dead.

They were scientists engaged in an experiment instead.
 'There's an island, little rodent, you'll live on alone.
We'll study your behaviour for a scientific paper.'
 They slid a small radio under Razza's skin. (**OUCH!**)
You couldn't really see it because it was thinner than
thin. But it was powerful and strong, bouncing signals
over distances long, to a satellite way up high in the sky
and back to the scientists standing by.
 'What do you think of that?' the scientists asked.
'Aren't you proud to be able to help us in our task?'

'Well, I wouldn't say I was crazy about it,' said Razza.

In *The Daily Mouse Gazette* the rat elders read of Razza's sad fate.

'Alas and alack, he'll never be back.' They waved him goodbye as away he went to that lonely old island where he had been sent.

Day after day Razza would stray, week after week his outlook was bleak.

Weeks turned into months and the scientists were happy, but Razza himself was not a happy chappy.

'Oh bother, bother, belly button,' he grumbled as he sniffed and he stumbled, from hilltop to beach, looking across to the mainland way out of reach.

Now what would you do, if your only companions were a mouldy seagull or two? Wouldn't you get bored after the whole island you'd explored? No cat to scare out of its whiskers? No human to frighten out of his britches? No elders to tease as the cheese you did ease from the trap, until with a sneeze, you made it snap? Oh, it had been so funny to see the elders die of fright, what a sight!

'I'm getting out of here,' Razza said. He made the decision to escape from his prison.

'World, here I come!'

Part Two

Razza's amazing adventures began. He dived into the sea and he **swam** and he **swam**.

He did mousestroke mostly but, whenever he was tired, he **FLIPPED** onto his back before all his strength expired.

The scientists tracking him asked, 'Where can he be?' What a commotion when they discovered he was in the sea!

'DRAT! Catch that rat!'

Razza evaded them all in a sudden squall.

'CAN'T CATCH ME!'

But then he disappeared off the screen. For three days no PING was to be seen.

Do you want to know what happened to Razza?

Now, girls and boys, dry your eyes for here is the big surprise: Razza didn't drown.

Instead, in the dark he did bump into something, which turned out to be an albatross's rump.

'**Oops, sorry,**' Razza said, as he swallowed some water. '**Please excuse me.**'

The bird was called **Albie** (short for Albert, which he'd disliked ever since he was a little squirt).

'With all the space in the sea and you bump into me?' he asked. 'What are you doing out here little rat?'

'I think this is called drowning,' Razza spluttered.

'Bye now. Catch you later,' he barely uttered.

But Albie was a nice albatross and took pity on the
wet rat so far from the city. 'Alley-oop,' he said, and
Razza was on his back. Albie did a running streak
across the waves and then with a mighty spring he took
wing, lifting high,

FLYING ALL THE WAY RIGHT UP TO THE SKY!

'Thank you, Albie,' Razza said, 'I could have died.'
And as the sun dried him out his radio revived. PING!
The scientists were amazed and happily raved —

'RAZZA'S STILL ALIVE!'

They tracked him on their computer screen. The
map looked familiar. No one could believe their eyes.

'RAZZA HAS REACHED THE COAST OF AUSTRALIA!'

RAZZA THE RAT
CROSSES THE TASMAN!

THE DAILY MOUSE GAZETTE published photographs
sent by pigeon post across the ocean.

Razza was the sensation of the mouse nation.

The rat elders, however, still held dire fears. When
they heard Australian Customs wouldn't let him into
their country, they pricked up their ears.

'How will he get back home?' they asked. 'This is
what happens to rats who roam.'

But was Razza thinking of going back home?

Nah.

'Why go home when I've come this far?' He shook
Albie's wing goodbye.

'Tally-ho,' Albie said, flying into the sky. 'Off
I go, winging low! Go well, little rat!'

Razza stayed with some cuzzies on the GOLD COAST. He got a tan and ate some shrimps off their barbecue roast. But one day, wandering by the sea, Razza was again bored out of his tree. A newspaper came blowing past and what did **Razza see?**

The word: **JAPAN.**

Do you know the saying, children, 'Curiosity killed the cat'? The same can apply to a curious rat.

'I've always wanted to go there,' he said, 'and climb Mt Fuji, a beautiful mountain that should be lovely this summer.'

The PING started pinging as Razza went swimming.

'He's on the move again, boys,' the scientists yelled with surprise. 'That little rascal rat! **WOW**, where's Razza off to now?'

Razza dived into the sea and he **SWAM** and he **SWAM**. He did mousestroke mostly but, whenever he was tired, he **FLIPPED** onto his back before all his strength expired. And he was feeling happy to be on his travels again but ...

Oh girls and boys, whenever you read the paper make sure you read the lot because this is the part that Razza had **NOT** got:

JAPAN FEARS TSUNAMI.

So close your eyes, children, if you don't want to know what happened to RAZZA when the wind began to blow. Don't peek between your fingers, oh dear me, or you may see a poor little rat drowning in the sea.

The storm began to shriek. The waves began to peak. The gales began to howl. The squall was very, very foul. The tsunami was now full force, throwing Razza completely off course! Nothing could survive that, least of all a little rat.

(Say goodbye to Razza, girls and boys.)

27

'Oh bother, bother, belly button,'

Razza said as he went down for
the last time in all that horrible
seawater and saltwater slime.

'Goodbye,
dear world.'

But, **AHA**, he suddenly remembered his old Granny rat who once told him, 'Razza, if ever you're lost at sea, call your ancestor and ask, **'Rescue me.'**

And so, just before he passed out, Razza gave a cry and, before he knew what was happening, he was carried high by something that was ...

Bigger than **big**. **Huger** than **huge**.

Taller than tall.

WIDER than **WIDE!**

Okay, girls and boys, you can open your eyes and
dry your tears.

What do you think it was?

That's right! It was a whale, huge and jolly, and his
name turned out to be **Wally!**

'You called, Bro?'

'Oh,' Razza said meekly. 'I hope I didn't disturb you.'

'Don't dismay,' said Wally, 'Which way are you
heading? To Japan? Okay, hold on tight, cuz, we're on
the way!'

RAZZA THE WHALE RIDER ARRIVES IN JAPAN!

You can imagine the cheers that greeted the news when The Daily Mouse Gazette published bird's-eye views of Razza's arrival in Tokyo Harbour.

Even the rat elders gave gruff approval when they saw Razza's photo as he toured Kyoto and when, that summer, he climbed Mt Fuji.

But still they cautioned the young ones: 'While it's okay to be a rebel, your problems can **treble**. Best to have a safe life because, that way, you'll have no strife. And who knows, for all the adventures to which RAZZA does aspire, around the next corner he might be out of the frying pan and into the *fire!*'

Well, lucky for us, Razza kept on making a fuss.

He didn't care about the rat elders back home and he kept on roaming, roaming his roam.

He hitched a ride on a plane flying west to the Himalayas, the highest mountains in the world.

'THIS IS SIMPLY THE BEST!'

he said as he climbed Everest.

34

He spent some time in those countries sublime,
Greece and Spain, where he scared the bullfighter in a
bullfight one day and saved the bull from his sword,

'OLÉ!'

He ratpacked through France and climbed the
Eiffel Tower. Then he donned warm flannel for a swim
across the Channel.

Thank you, Razza!

He dived into the sea and he **SWAM** and he **SWAM**.
He did mousestroke mostly but, whenever he was tired,
he **FLIPPED** onto his back before all his strength
expired.

If ever any adversity came his way, do you remember
what he would say?

That's right!

'Oh bother, bother, belly button.'

And the scientists, tracking him, would say, 'WOW! Where's that Razza off to now?'

Razza visited the Tower and went on the London Eye.
On a visit to Buckingham Palace he did spy a tomcat
sitting under the Queen's chair.

'Squeak!' he squeaked, and the tomcat shrieked.

'I always wanted to do that,' Razza said.

Wherever he went he made the headlines in The
Daily Mouse Gazette. He was interviewed in London.

Squeak!

'My adventures,' said Razza, 'are not over yet.'

Queen Honours New Zealand
Rat with Mousehood

From England, Razza caught an iceberg sailing west across the Atlantic. But it was so sunny that something funny happened to the ice. Before he could think twice, the iceberg melted away — things were looking pretty DICEY.

He dived into the sea and he SWAM and he SWAM. He did mousestroke mostly but, when he was tired, he FLIPPED onto his back before all his energy expired.

The sea was freezing and poor Razza was
w h e e z i n g.

At home in New Zealand the rat elders were sad.
'He'll never make it,' they said as they prepared for
bed.

Even the scientists watching his PING on the screen
saw that it was slowing. 'Poor Razza he's tiring, poor
Razza's expiring.' But ...

'I've got fur!' Razza realised. 'It's like a coat that
will keep me warm as I swim across this moat!'

He struck out again, swimming and swimming. The
scientists cheered as his PING kept on pinging. Now how
many rats could ever boast that they had swum to the
Texan coast?

Razza, first rat to
swim the Atlantic

Part Three

Boys and girls, gather close as I tell you the story of how Razza achieved his greatest glory.

While in London having tea and cake with the Queen, on television he had seen that America was sending a manned rocket to the moon. The news made him swoon.

'Bye bye Queenie,' he said as he sped to the sea, 'that space rocket's not going without me!'

The plain fact was that the earth was too small for this adventurous rat — space was where all the ACTION was at!

On arrival in Texas Razza hitched a ride from Houston's downtown — some humans were heading for the space rocket's final countdown.

When he got to Canaveral (Cape), the sight of the rocket left Razza agape.

'OH, WOW!' Razza gasped.

The rocket was ready, a sight so sublime and Razza, well, he'd arrived just in time.

Now, hush, girls and boys, don't make a sound.
Razza has to get through **SECURITY** before he is found.

He went through **NO ENTRY** and he was so small that armed guards didn't pick him up at all. When he saw **AUTHORISED PERSONNEL ONLY** he gave his tail a swish and pretended, 'Me no speaka da English.'

He made it unscathed **(Phew!)** as far as the stairs. 'Do I have to climb up there?' he asked in despair.

As he scampered up the tower he saw a gull glower.
'Going somewhere, bud?' said the gull, full of power.
But Razza would **not** be stopped. 'Get out of my way,' he said with a ROAR. Man, you should have seen that gull soar!

Razza made it! When the astronauts walked into the rocket, guess who was there in one of their pockets! (Heh! Heh! Heh!)

The rocket was ...

bigger than big.

Huger than huge.

Taller than tall.

WIDER than **WIDE.**

Nobody knew that Razza the Rat had sneaked inside.

The countdown began and Razza's heart went **thumpity-thump**. His four knees each went bumpity-bump. His tiny white teeth went clickety-click and clickety-clack.

'I'm feeling sick,' Razza said. 'I'm going back.'

But it was too late. He'd already sealed his Fate.

'Oh bother, bother, belly button.'

With a thunderous roar the engines started and the spaceship departed. It shook and it boomed as away it zoomed. It rose high into the stratosphere, and earth dwindled away.

And didn't the scientists go white when it zoomED past their satellite? What dismay!

Because here's the thing: as it went by it gave a huge PING!

'WOW! Where's Razza off to now?'

Very soon pictures came back of the astronauts on the moon.

And who was that standing far below, next to an **ASTRONAUT'S TOE?**

It was Razza grinning like mad and waving a small rat flag.

RAZZA, FIRST RAT ON THE MOON!

Tḥe Dɑḡly Mouse Gɑᴏette carried the news. It was so wonderful that the rat elders changed their views.

'We **always** knew Razza would do it,' they said. 'When he was young we knew in a trice that he'd bring honour and glory to all of us mice. If you stay in your house you'll be a timorous mouse. If from your mouseholes you never venture, you will never be able to have an **adventure**.'

Hadn't they changed their tune!

So, children, time for bed and to rest your weary heads. Let's raise a cheer as RAZZA'S adventures are told far and near. And as you swim through your dreams to Venus or Mars, just remember that your journey's not over until you reach the stars!

Can you help Razza find his hat?

Author's Note

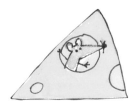

The Amazing Adventures of Razza the Rat was inspired by a real rat that was part of an experiment conducted by PhD student James Russell, the University of Auckland and the Department of Conservation, New Zealand.

The rat was fitted with a radio-tracking collar and released onto the uninhabited island of Motuhoropapa in the Noises Group. He was monitored for four weeks and astounded everybody by swimming nearly half a kilometre to neighbouring Otata Island, where he was captured 18 weeks later. His feat was published in top magazines and newspapers around the world. This was the longest distance recorded for a rat swimming across open sea.

About the author

Witi Ihimaera was born in Gisborne, New Zealand, and now lives in Auckland. After early work as a labourer and postman while beginning his writing career, he has had a distinguished career as a diplomat and university lecturer. His first book was *Pounamu Pounamu*, a collection of short stories. *The Amazing Adventures of Razza the Rat* is his third book written for children. Witi has published many novels for adults and collections of short stories, as well as writing plays and opera. He is world-famous for his novel *The Whale Rider* (now in over 20 editions worldwide), which was made into a film and released in 2003. In 2005, Witi revised *The Whale Rider* so it could be published as a children's picture book.

About the illustrator

Astrid Matijasevich is a graphic design graduate who has been working in the publishing industry as an illustrator for the past 20 years. She shares her Auckland home with her partner and their two teenage boys, and a Siamese cat called Diesel.

This is her first collaboration with the author.

Don't forget to visit your local bookshop
or
www.reed.co.nz
to see more great children's books from
Reed Publishing!